THE HALLOWEEN TREE

Words by Susan Montanari
Pictures by Teresa Martinez

sourcebooks
jabberwocky

With love to Jennifer, Danielle, Laura, and The Tree! –SM

To my sweet dear friend, Dulce. –TM

Text © 2019 by Susan Montanari
Illustrations © 2019 by Teresa Martinez
Cover and internal design © 2019 by Sourcebooks

Sourcebooks and the colophon are registered trademarks of Sourcebooks, Inc.

The artwork was created digitally using Photoshop and a Wacom tablet.

Published by Sourcebooks Jabberwocky, an imprint of Sourcebooks Kids
P.O. Box 4410, Naperville, Illinois 60567-4410
(630) 961-3900
sourcebookskids.com

Library of Congress Cataloging-in-Publication Data
is on file with the publisher.

Source of Production: Leo Paper, Heshan City, Guangdong Province, China
Date of Production: March 2021
Run Number: 5021471

Printed and bound in China.
LEO 10 9 8 7 6 5 4 3 2

The Christmas tree farm bustled with excitement. Carols played as families moved up and down the rows of tall pine trees, exclaiming, "This one is beautiful," or "That one is perfect."

Looking at the fancy, decorated tree at the front, one sapling grumbled, "I don't like lights, I don't like decorations, and I don't like people."

As trees disappeared off the lot, the little tree
mumbled, "I don't want to be a Christmas tree.
I never want to leave this spot."

The little tree listened as the other saplings buzzed with anticipation.
"I can't wait," a sprout whispered.
"Colored lights," one sighed.
"I hope I get a star on my top," said another.

The little tree grumbled. "I don't want to become a Christmas tree, and I'm not going to."

As the little tree grew, its limbs became gnarled and twisted. Every time needles sprouted, thoughts of being decorated with lights and ornaments made them turn brown and fall off.

The tree looked nothing like the others.

One day, all the trees on the lot disappeared.
All except one.

Eventually, houses began to appear, and with houses came families.
By then the tree had grown tall and broad. Its limbs were twisted and
covered with strange knobs.

One summer, the tree heard children's voices coming near and scoffed, "Ugh…people."

"Yikes," a boy named Ben cried.
"That tree looks gruuummpy."

"I like it," his sister Sarah said as she touched a branch.

"It's so creepy. I dare you to climb it," their friend Tomas challenged her.

Sarah pulled herself up into the tree and sat on a cozy bough.

"It's a pirate ship," she shouted and waved for the others to join her. All the children climbed aboard.

When the neighborhood kids needed a hideout, the tree became their fort.

When they played astronauts and aliens, it was their spaceship.

NO Parents allowed

And one foggy day, the tree even turned into a dragon.

When winter came, a cold wind blew, and the children didn't come outside to play.

The tree, with its limbs empty, stood all alone.

On a snowy afternoon, the tree watched as Sarah and Ben's father carried a large bundle into the house. That night, a Christmas tree appeared in the window.

"I don't like lights, I don't like decorations, and I don't like people," the tree whispered, but it couldn't turn away.

The next year the same
thing happened. The kids
played in the branches until
the snow began to fall.

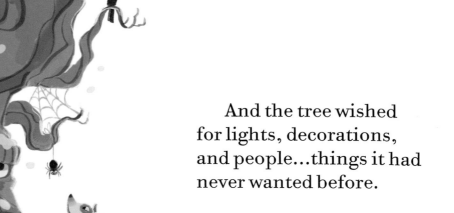

And the tree wished
for lights, decorations,
and people…things it had
never wanted before.

One spring, the tree tried to make its needles grow properly, but after years of trying to stop them, they came in looking all wrong.

By summer, they had fallen off.

A few months later, Sarah and Ben's parents were decorating for Halloween. Their father looked across the yard and said, "That is one horrible old tree."

"We should cut it down," their mother agreed.

Not now, the tree thought. *Not now that my limbs are full* of happy children.

Up in the branches, Sarah whispered, "No, they can't."
"We have to save our tree," Tomas cried.
"I know what to do," Ben said and whispered his plan to the other kids.
They climbed down and raced away to gather supplies.

When they came back, Ben was already up in the tree wedging a huge jack-o'-lantern in a nook. They all climbed up, and from the tree's branches they hung white and orange lights, cobwebs made from string, rubber spiders, cardboard cats and bats, ghosts, witches, and skeletons.

That night the parents and all the
neighbors gathered to admire the tree.
     The children danced beneath, shouting,
"Trick or tree!" to each other.

I guess I was wrong, the tree thought, *I do like lights. I do like decorations, and I do like people. I love being a Halloween tree!*